JE BERENSTAIN
Berenstain, Stan,
The Berenstain bears and the spooky
old tree /

Bright and Early Books

Bright and Early Books are an offspring of the world-famous Beginner Books . . . designed for *an even lower age group*. Making ingenious use of humor, rhythm and limited vocabulary, they will encourage even pre-schoolers to discover the delights of reading for themselves.

For other Bright and Early titles see the back endpapers.

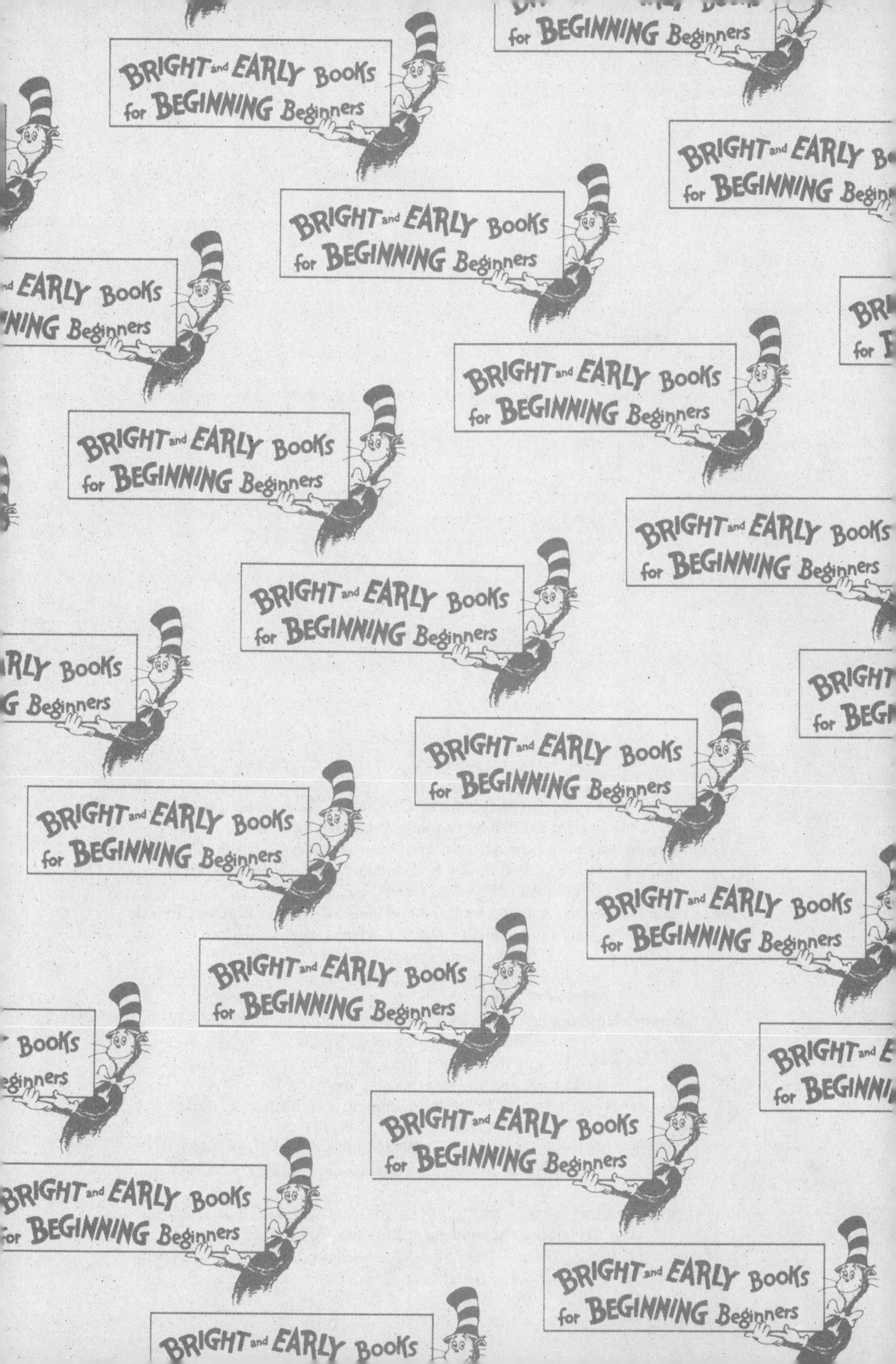
BRIGHT and EARLY BOOKS
for BEGINNING Beginners

Library of Congress Cataloging-in-Publication Data:
Berenstain, Stanley. The Berenstain bears and the spooky old tree.
(A Bright and early book; BE23)
SUMMARY: One by one, three brave little bears have second thoughts
about exploring the interior of a spooky old tree.
[1. Bears—Fiction.] I. Berenstain, Janice, joint author. II. Title.
PZ7.B4483Bek [E] 77-93771
ISBN: 0-394-83910-2 (trade) — ISBN: 0-394-93910-7 (lib. bdg.)
Printed in the United States of America
53

A Bright & Early Book

THE BERENSTAIN BEARS AND THE SPOOKY OLD TREE

Stan and Jan Berenstain

m BEGINNER BOOKS   A Division of Random House, Inc.

Three little bears.

One with a light.
One with a stick.
One with a rope.

A spooky old tree.

Yes.
They dare.

Three little bears...
One with a light.
One with a stick.
One with a rope.

A twisty old stair.

Do they dare go up
that twisty old stair?

Yes.
They dare.

Three little bears.
One with a light.
One with a stick.
And <u>one</u> with the shivers.

A giant key.

A moving wall.

Will the three little bears
go through that wall?
Do they dare go into
that spooky old hall?

Yes.
They dare.

Three little bears.
One with a light.
And <u>two</u> with the shivers.

Great Sleeping Bear.

Do they dare go over
Great Sleeping Bear?

Do they dare?
Well…

They came into the tree.

They climbed the stair.

They went through the wall...

and into the hall.

So of course they went over
Great Sleeping Bear!

Three little bears...
without a light,
without a stick,
without a rope.
And <u>all</u> with the shivers!

How will they ever
get out of there?

Three little bears
running fast.

Home again.
Safe at last.

Stan & Jan Berenstain

began writing and illustrating books for children in the early 1960s, when their two young sons, Michael and Leo, were beginning to read. They live on a hillside in Bucks County, Pennsylvania, a place that looks a lot like Bear Country. They see deer, wild turkeys, rabbits, squirrels, and woodchucks through their studio window almost every day—but no bears. The Bears live inside their hearts and minds.

The Berenstains' sons are all grown up now. Michael is an illustrator. Leo is a writer. Stan and Jan have four grandchildren. One of them can already draw pretty good bears. With more than two hundred books in print, along with videos, television shows, and even Berenstain Bears attractions at major amusement parks, it's hard to tell where the Bears end and the Berenstains begin!

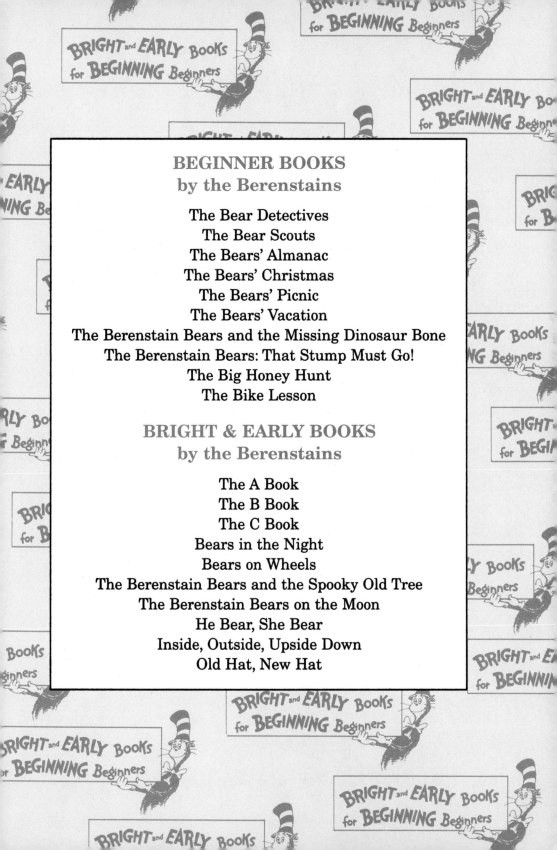

BEGINNER BOOKS
by the Berenstains

The Bear Detectives
The Bear Scouts
The Bears' Almanac
The Bears' Christmas
The Bears' Picnic
The Bears' Vacation
The Berenstain Bears and the Missing Dinosaur Bone
The Berenstain Bears: That Stump Must Go!
The Big Honey Hunt
The Bike Lesson

BRIGHT & EARLY BOOKS
by the Berenstains

The A Book
The B Book
The C Book
Bears in the Night
Bears on Wheels
The Berenstain Bears and the Spooky Old Tree
The Berenstain Bears on the Moon
He Bear, She Bear
Inside, Outside, Upside Down
Old Hat, New Hat